RAINBOW magic

The Party Fairies

To a very special Jasmine -
Miss Jasmine Grewal - with lots of love

Special thanks to
Narinder Dhami

ORCHARD BOOKS
338 Euston Road, London NW1 3BH
Orchard Books Australia
Hachette Children's Books
Level 17/207 Kent Street, Sydney, NSW 2000
A Paperback Original
First published in Great Britain in 2005
Rainbow Magic is a registered trademark of Working Partners Limited.
Series created by Working Partners Limited, London W6 OQT
Text © Working Partners Limited 2005
Illustrations © Georgie Ripper 2005
The right of Georgie Ripper to be identified as the illustrator
of this work has been asserted by her in accordance
with the Copyright, Designs and Patents Act, 1988.
A CIP catalogue record for this book is available
from the British Library.
ISBN 1 84362 824 4
9 10 8
Printed in Great Britain

Jasmine
the Present Fairy

by Daisy Meadows

illustrated by Georgie Ripper

ORCHARD BOOKS

www.rainbowmagic.co.uk

A Very Special Party Invitation

Our gracious King and gentle Queen
Are loved by fairies all.
One thousand years have they ruled well,
Through troubles great and small.

In honour of their glorious reign
A party has been planned,
To celebrate their jubilee
Throughout all Fairyland.

The party is a royal surprise,
We hope they'll be delighted.
So shine your wand and press your dress...
For you have been invited!

RSVP: HRH THE FAIRY GODMOTHER

Contents

A Special Street Party   9

Unlucky Dip!   23

Girls on the Run   35

All Wrapped Up   47

Fairyland Fun   53

Party Time!   65

A Special Street Party

"Look at all these stalls, Rachel," Kirsty Tate said, pointing down the street where she lived. "This is going to be a great party!"

All of Kirsty's neighbours were bustling around setting up stalls outside their houses. There were all sorts of things going on, from games and raffles

to stalls selling bric-a-brac and cakes.
Delicious smells wafted towards the
girls, from the barbecue at the other
end of the street. The road was closed
to traffic, and people were already
milling around in the sunshine,
enjoying the fête.

"I think having a street party is
a great idea," Rachel Walker,
Kirsty's best friend, said with a grin.
"I wish we had one in our street
back home." Rachel had come to
stay with Kirsty for a week of the
Easter holidays.

Kirsty was opening the last box of books. "We'd better hurry and put these on the stall," she said. "Lots of people are arriving now."

"I'm glad the party is today, before I go home tomorrow," Rachel said, helping Kirsty arrange the books on the stall that Mr and Mrs Tate were running. "I hope we raise loads of money for charity."

"We always do," said Kirsty happily, stacking the books neatly. "Lots of people come to the party from all over town. But..." she lowered her voice, "...we'll have to be extra-careful this year, won't we?"

Rachel nodded solemnly. "Yes," she agreed. "A party means we must keep our eyes open for goblin mischief!"

Rachel and Kirsty shared a wonderful secret. They had become friends with the fairies and now, whenever their fairy friends were in trouble, Rachel and Kirsty were happy to help. The cause of the trouble was usually cold, spiky Jack Frost, who had been banished to his ice castle by the King and Queen of Fairyland. This time Jack Frost was determined to ruin the secret party which the Fairy Godmother and the seven Party Fairies were planning for the Fairy King and Queen's 1000th jubilee.

Jack Frost had sent his mean goblin servants into the human world to spoil as many parties as they could.

When the Party Fairies flew to the rescue, the goblins tried to steal their magic party bags so that Jack Frost could use their special magic to throw a fabulous party of his own! But Rachel and Kirsty had managed to stop the goblins so far, and help six of the Party Fairies to keep their party bags safe.

"I'm not going to let Jack Frost's goblins spoil our street party," Kirsty said in a determined voice. "Or the King and Queen's jubilee."

Rachel nodded in agreement as Kirsty's parents hurried towards them.

"You have done well," Mrs Tate smiled, admiring the neat piles of books.

"I think you two girls have worked hard enough," Mr Tate added, as customers began to gather round the stall. "You can go and explore the fête."

"Great!" Kirsty whispered to Rachel, as they walked away. "Now we've got a chance to look for goblins!"

The girls wandered happily through the crowds. There were lots of games, such as darts, hook-a-duck and a tombola, and there were tables piled with bric-a-brac, toys, home-made jams, and other things for sale.

Rachel stopped at a cake stall, her mouth watering as she looked at the delicious display of tarts, sponges and pies. "Cherry the Cake Fairy would be proud of those," she laughed.

"There's no sign of any goblin mischief," said Kirsty. "Shall we have a go on the tombola?"

The tombola was manned by one of Kirsty's neighbours, Mr Cooper, and there was already a queue. Kirsty and Rachel stood behind a little girl holding her mum's hand.

The girl was staring up at the prizes on the shelves behind the tombola machine. "I hope I win a cuddly toy, Mummy," she said excitedly.

"Any ticket ending in four wins a prize!" called Mr Cooper, spinning the tombola round.

Rachel and Kirsty watched as the little girl pulled out a purple ticket. She unfolded it carefully.

"Mummy, I won!" she gasped. "It's number 214."

"Well done!" her mum laughed.

"Let's hope it's a soft toy," Rachel whispered to Kirsty, as the little girl handed Mr Cooper the ticket.

But sharp-eyed Kirsty had already spotted the prize with purple ticket 214 pinned to it. "It's not," she said, pointing. "Look."

The prize was a blue, plastic apron
with a picture of a fluffy, white kitten
on the front. Kirsty hoped the little girl
wouldn't be too disappointed.

"Right, let me find your prize," said
Mr Cooper, scanning the shelves. "It's
here somewhere…"

But just before he spotted the apron,
something magical happened. Rachel
and Kirsty saw a shower
of blue sparkles appear
from thin air and whirl
around the apron. The
next moment, the apron
had vanished and in its
place sat a fluffy, white
toy kitten, with a blue satin
bow around its neck. Pinned to
the bow was purple ticket 214.

"I've won the white kitten!" the little girl cried joyfully.

Looking puzzled, Mr Cooper lifted the toy down. "I don't remember seeing that prize before," he murmured.

Kirsty and Rachel grinned at each other as Mr Cooper handed the kitten to the delighted little girl.

"That was fairy magic," whispered Kirsty.

Rachel nodded. "And that means there must be a Party Fairy very nearby!"

Unlucky Dip!

The little girl skipped off happily, clutching her prize, while Kirsty and Rachel slipped behind the tombola stall to look for the fairy. They couldn't see any sign of her.

"Rachel! Kirsty!" The girls suddenly heard a silvery voice calling from above their heads. "I'm up here!"

The girls looked up at a string of coloured flags tied to the top of the stall, and there was Jasmine the Present Fairy, balancing on the string like an acrobat on a tightrope!

"Hello," Kirsty and Rachel called, smiling up at her.

Jasmine fluttered
down to join them,
her straight brown
hair flying out behind
her. She wore a long,
blue skirt with a fluted
hemline that swirled around
her ankles, and a cropped top in the
same shade of blue. On her feet were
dark blue ballet shoes with satin ribbons,
and in her hand she carried a glittering
blue wand.

"I'm here to make sure that your street
party goes well," she explained, "and
that all the prizes are as perfect as
possible." She smiled at Rachel and
Kirsty. "And that means making sure no
naughty goblins try to ruin the party!"
she added in a determined voice.

"Have you seen any goblins?" Rachel asked anxiously.

"No—" Jasmine began, but she was interrupted by the sound of someone crying loudly. It came from the lucky dip, next to the tombola.

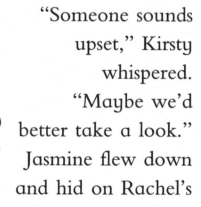

"Someone sounds upset," Kirsty whispered. "Maybe we'd better take a look." Jasmine flew down and hid on Rachel's shoulder behind her hair. Then they hurried over to join the queue at the lucky dip. A little boy was standing by the bran tub, crying bitterly with a toy plane in his hand.

"I loved the plane when I unwrapped it," the boy wailed. "But look, Dad, the wings are broken!"

"This could be goblin trouble," Jasmine whispered in Rachel's ear.

"I'm very sorry," said the man at the lucky dip stall. "I tell you what, why don't you pull out another parcel for free?"

The boy stopped crying immediately. "Thank you," he beamed.

Rachel, Kirsty and Jasmine watched as
the little boy put his hand
into the bran tub
and pulled out
a small parcel.
He unwrapped
it eagerly, but
they all stared
in horror when
a mouldy, old
apple fell out!

"Oh, no!" Jasmine gasped.

The little boy began to cry again.

Meanwhile, the stallholder was
looking very flustered. "I think
somebody's playing a silly joke on
me!" he said crossly. "Don't cry." He
patted the little boy on the shoulder.
"Have another go."

Rachel, Kirsty and Jasmine watched
anxiously as the boy
pulled out his third
parcel. This time he
unwrapped a toy car
without any wheels!

"All the presents in
the lucky dip are
spoiled," Kirsty whispered to
Rachel and Jasmine. "What are we
going to do?"

The little boy was about to burst into
tears again, but the kind stallholder
saved the day.

"Look," he said, leaning across to the
hook-a-duck stall next door, which he
was also running. "I'll give you one of
these prizes instead." And he handed
the boy a shiny bat and ball set.

"Great!" the boy said happily, showing it to his dad as they walked away.

"This is definitely goblin mischief!" Jasmine said as the man bent over the bran tub and began looking through it. "But I'll soon set things right with my party magic."

"That's exactly what the goblin will be hoping for," Kirsty hissed, looking worried. "Don't get your party bag out – he'll be waiting for a chance to steal it!"

"I can't help that," Jasmine whispered, glancing at the boys and girls behind them. "The children will be so disappointed if I don't fix the lucky dip."

"Well, we'll help," Rachel said. "Kirsty, let's make sure the stall owner doesn't notice Jasmine at work. And keep your eyes peeled for goblins."

The man was looking very glum. "I don't think you should have a go, girls," he said. "I may have to close the lucky dip."

"No, don't do that," Rachel said quickly. "I'd like a go on your hook-a-duck stall. What do I have to do?"

31

While the man was talking to Rachel, Jasmine slid quietly off her shoulder and flew down to the edge of the bran tub. Meanwhile, Kirsty stood right in front of the tub so that nobody in the queue could see what was happening. She was looking out for goblins too.

Quickly, Jasmine opened her party bag and took out a handful of sparkling blue fairy dust, shaped like tiny bows. She sprinkled it over the bran tub and gave a sigh of relief. "All done!" she whispered to Kirsty.

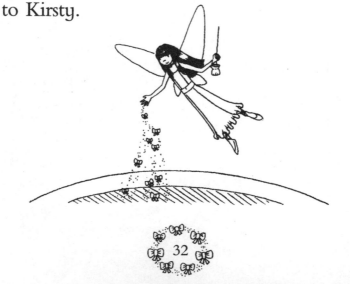

But just then there was a scrabbling noise from *inside* the bran tub. Suddenly, a big green goblin popped up and snatched at Jasmine's party bag.

Girls on the Run

"Oh!" Jasmine and Kirsty gasped together as the goblin lunged towards them.

Luckily, Jasmine was too quick for him and she whisked the party bag out of his reach. Muttering crossly, the goblin leapt out of the bran tube and darted out of sight behind the stall.

Still shaking with fright, Jasmine
fluttered up to sit on Kirsty's
shoulder but as she
landed, her party
bag slipped from
her trembling
fingers. It fell
straight into the
lucky dip and
disappeared amidst the sawdust.

"Oh, no!" Kirsty groaned.

Over the shoulder of the stallholder,
Rachel had seen what was happening.
Somehow they had to get Jasmine's
party bag back – and fast. "Er,
actually I don't want a go on the
hook-a-duck," she said quickly. "I
think I'll have a go on the lucky dip,
after all."

The man looked amazed. "Are you sure?" he asked. "It doesn't seem very lucky at the moment."

"Quite sure," Rachel said firmly.

"Me too," Kirsty added, guessing what Rachel was up to.

The two girls handed over their money. Kirsty went first and Rachel, Jasmine and the stallholder watched as she felt around inside the tub. Her fingers closed over something and she pulled it out. But it was one of the wrapped presents, not Jasmine's party bag. Inside the parcel was a beautiful blue mini-kite.

"At least the presents are OK now," Jasmine whispered in Kirsty's ear.

"Your turn," said the stallholder, looking at Rachel. But just then one of the children at the hook-a-duck stall  gave a cry of alarm. He had accidentally got his fishing-rod caught in a string of flags! The stallholder went to help, and Rachel leaned over the bran tub. But just as Rachel was making her lucky dip, Kirsty gave a gasp of horror.

"Watch out!" she whispered. "The goblin is climbing up the table leg!"

Sure enough, the goblin was clambering up the leg of the table back towards the bran tub, with a very determined look on his face.

"There's only your dip left, Rachel," Kirsty whispered anxiously. "You must get Jasmine's party bag before the goblin does!"

Quickly, Rachel plunged her hand into the sawdust and began to feel around. She wondered how she would know when she'd found the party bag, but then she felt something tingle under her fingers. "Fairy magic!" Rachel said to herself, and she drew the object out.

Both girls gasped with relief – it was Jasmine's party bag.

"Hurrah!" Jasmine cried happily.

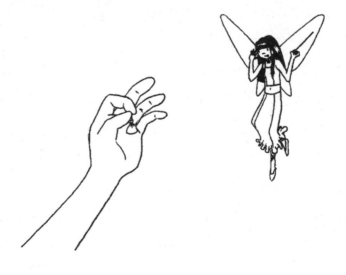

"Thanks, Rachel."

Just then the goblin peered
over the edge of the
bran tub. He
grinned when
he saw the party
bag and made
another grab
for it, but Rachel
managed to jump
away from him, clutching
the bag tightly.

"Let's get out of here," Kirsty
suggested. "Quick, back
to my house!"

The girls and Jasmine darted behind
the stall and ran away from the fête
towards the Tates' house. But the
goblin chased after them.

Rachel glanced over her shoulder. "He's not far behind!" she panted.

They reached the house and Kirsty let them in through the front door. But the goblin was charging towards them and the girls only just managed to slam the door shut in time. "We have to get rid of that goblin," Jasmine said urgently.

"I've got an idea!"
Kirsty declared suddenly. "Rachel, you
guard the door. Jasmine,
follow me."

Rachel nodded and
waited by the front
door as Jasmine and
Kirsty dashed into
the living-room.

Then a tiny sound
made Rachel jump.

Her heart thumping, Rachel looked
round. She smiled to see Pearl, Kirsty's
black and white kitten, sitting at the
top of the stairs, watching her.

But then Rachel heard something else.
It was the noise of the catflap in the
kitchen door creaking open. Rachel
frowned. If Pearl was sitting on the
stairs, then who was coming in?

She crept along the hall towards the
kitchen and spotted...the goblin,
climbing in through the catflap.

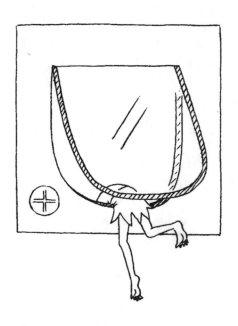

"Kirsty! Jasmine!" she shouted. "Look out, the goblin's coming!"

All Wrapped Up

In the living-room, Jasmine looked at Kirsty in alarm. "What shall we do?" she cried.

But Kirsty was picking up an empty cardboard box which had been full of books for the stall. "If we can make the goblin believe your party bag is in this box, we might be able to trap him inside!" she said.

"Can you lay a trail of magic sparkles leading into the box?"

"I can do better than that!" Jasmine replied eagerly. She opened her party bag and sprinkled some glittering fairy dust onto the cardboard. Immediately, it changed into a beautiful blue gift box, with a lovely golden ribbon lying beside it. Then Jasmine laid the trail of fairy dust into the box and she and Kirsty dived out of sight behind the sofa.

No sooner were Kirsty
and Jasmine in hiding
than the goblin
dashed into the
living-room
and skidded to
a halt, closely
followed by Rachel.

Poor Rachel couldn't
believe her eyes when she
saw the trail of fairy dust and no sign
of Kirsty and Jasmine. "Oh, no!" she
gasped. "If the party bag is in the box,
the goblin can take it!"

The goblin had also spotted the fairy
dust trail and he was beaming all over
his face. "Ha!" he chuckled gleefully,
sticking his tongue out at Rachel. "Jack
Frost is going to be very pleased with me

when I take him a magic party bag!"
And, still chuckling, he crawled into
the box.

Immediately, Jasmine and Kirsty rushed

out from behind
the sofa. Rachel,
who wasn't
expecting it,
almost jumped
out of her skin.
"Quick, Rachel!"
cried Kirsty,
"Help me
close the box!"

Rachel sprang forward,
and she and Kirsty shut the lid.
Then Jasmine waved her wand, and
the gold ribbon floated up into the air
and tied itself firmly around the box.

There was a cry of rage from inside as the goblin realised he'd been tricked.

"So that's what you were up to!" Rachel laughed.

"Let me out!" the goblin roared.

"I don't think so," Kirsty replied.

"Shall we send the goblin back to Jack Frost by fairy magic mail?" Jasmine suggested.

The girls nodded and Jasmine waved her wand again. There was a shower of fairy dust and a label appeared on the box. It said "Jack Frost, Ice Castle" in big letters. Then, in another swirl of glittering magic, the parcel vanished completely.

Fairyland Fun

Kirsty turned to Rachel. "We did it!" she beamed. "We saved all the Party Fairies' magic party bags!"

"That means the jubilee party for our King and Queen can go ahead without any more trouble from Jack Frost," Jasmine declared happily. "And it's all thanks to you two."

Kirsty and Rachel grinned proudly at each other.

Then Kirsty stared. "Look!" she cried, pointing at the window.

A rainbow of shimmering colours was streaming through the glass. The girls blinked in wonder as one end of the beautiful rainbow came to rest on the floor beside them.

"It's the magic rainbow to take us to Fairyland!" Rachel breathed.

"Remember, Kirsty? Bertram said
the Fairy Godmother would send a
rainbow for us when it was time for
the jubilee party."

"Oh!" Kirsty gasped. "But we're not
ready! We haven't got our party
clothes on."

Jasmine laughed.
"Just step onto
the end of the
rainbow, girls,"
she told them.
"We Party Fairies
will soon sort you
out when you get
to Fairyland." She
waved her wand. "See
you very soon!" she called, as
she vanished in a swirl of glitter.

"Come on, Kirsty," Rachel said, taking her friend's hand.

Together, the girls stepped carefully into the rainbow. Immediately, there was a whooshing sound, and they were surrounded by glittering golden fairy dust as the rainbow whisked them away.

"Here they are!" called a joyful voice.

As the golden sparkles cleared, the girls found themselves in the Great Hall of the Party Workshop in Fairyland. They were already fairy-sized themselves, with glittering wings on their backs. And there was Jasmine and the other six Party Fairies smiling at them.

"Welcome to the party!" they cried.

"Wow!" Rachel exclaimed, looking round.

Last time the girls had been there, the Party Fairies had been busy with preparations, but now everything was ready. All the fairies were there to welcome the King and Queen, dressed in their best party outfits. Grace the Glitter Fairy had been busy decorating the hall with sparkling streamers, rainbow balloons and jewelled lanterns. There were also

tiny, white fairy lights strung all
over the ceiling. Rachel and
Kirsty had never seen
anything so beautiful.
In one corner, the frog
orchestra was playing
a cheerful tune. In
another, presents
were piled up,
all beautifully
wrapped by
Jasmine and tied
with satin bows in
rainbow colours.
There were bowls of
sweets placed here and
there, and on a golden
table stood a huge cake shaped
like the King and Queen's palace.

Rachel and Kirsty were amused to see the goblin who had tried to steal Cherry the Cake Fairy's party bag, fussing over the cake.

"Now don't touch the icing," he was telling the fairies standing round the table. "I spent ages making sure it looked exactly like the palace!"

"He seems to be enjoying himself," Rachel whispered to Kirsty.

"I'm so happy to see you, girls," the Fairy Godmother declared as she hurried towards them. Her green eyes shone with happiness and the jewels on her golden dress twinkled in the candlelight. "We're so grateful to you for making sure our party wasn't ruined by Jack Frost!" She  turned to Phoebe the Fashion Fairy. "I think Phoebe has something for you."

"I do!" Phoebe laughed. "How about some beautiful new dresses for the party, girls?"

"Oh, yes please!" Kirsty and Rachel cried together.

Phoebe smiled and threw a handful of sparkling fairy dust over them. Both girls closed their eyes.

Kirsty was the first to open them again. "Oh, Rachel!" she gasped. "These are the most beautiful dresses I've ever seen!"

Rachel opened her eyes to see Kirsty wearing a long, sparkling rose-pink and gold dress, with pink ballet shoes and a glittering pink tiara. Rachel wore the same, but her outfit was in shimmering lilac and silver. "Thank you, Phoebe—" the girls began.

But before they could say any more, a little fairy zoomed into the Great Hall, panting with excitement. "The King and Queen are here!" she cried.

Party Time!

Everyone began to talk at once, but the Fairy Godmother raised her wand for silence. "Now remember," she called, "when the King and Queen get out of their carriage, everybody shouts, 'SURPRISE!'"

Rachel, Kirsty and all the fairies crowded around the door.

A shining crystal carriage, pulled by six white unicorns and driven by Bertram, the frog footman, was making its way towards them. The carriage stopped and Bertram hopped down to open the door. Out stepped the Fairy King and Queen.

"SURPRISE!" shouted everybody – Rachel and Kirsty loudest of all.

The King and Queen looked puzzled

for a moment, but then they saw the golden banner which hung over the castle door: Congratulations to our beloved King Oberon and Queen Titania on their 1000th jubilee!

"Oh!" the Queen gasped, looking delighted. "How wonderful!"

"I think our Party Fairies have had a hand in this," the King beamed joyfully.

The Fairy Godmother stepped forward. "Welcome, King Oberon and Queen Titania!" she announced. "But the Party Fairies aren't the only ones who have helped to make this party special. We must also thank our friends, Rachel and Kirsty." And she turned to smile at the girls. "Once again they have saved us from Jack Frost's mischief.

"Thank you, girls," said the King warmly. "You must tell us the whole story later."

"You both look beautiful," the Queen added with a smile. "Now, let's forget all about Jack Frost, and enjoy the party!"

Rachel and Kirsty had never been to
such a party in their lives.
The frog orchestra
played catchy tunes,
specially created by
Melodie the Music
Fairy, and all the
fairies danced and
fluttered around like
colourful butterflies.

Then there were party
games, organised by Polly the
Party Fun Fairy: Pass the Magic Parcel,
Musical Magical Chairs and many more.

The sweets made by Honey the Sweet Fairy were so delicious that Rachel and Kirsty just couldn't stop eating the Strawberry Sparkles.

After the games, everyone gathered round to watch the King and Queen open their presents and then cut the wonderful cake, made by Cherry and iced by the goblin. All too soon, the party was over.

"I hope you've had a good time, girls," Queen Titania said, smiling at Rachel and Kirsty.

"It was great!" Rachel declared.

"The best party ever!" Kirsty added.

"It's time for you to go home now," the Queen went on. She waved her wand and a shimmering rainbow appeared beside them. "But before you go, I think the Party Fairies have something for you."

Jasmine and Cherry flew forward.

"These are from all of us!" Jasmine said, handing Kirsty a pink, sparkly party bag, while Cherry gave Rachel a lilac one.

"Don't look in them till you get home."

"Thank you," Kirsty and Rachel replied, waving at their friends. "See you again soon, we hope."

"Goodbye!" answered all the fairies.

And with the voices of their fairy friends ringing in their ears, the girls stepped into the rainbow. Moments later, they found themselves in the Tates' kitchen, restored to their usual size and wearing their normal clothes once more.

"Oh, that was magical!"
Kirsty sighed happily.

Rachel was already
opening her party bag.
"Look, Kirsty!" she
exclaimed in delight.

The bags were full
of presents from their
Party Fairy friends.
There was a piece of jubilee
cake from Cherry, a fairy music CD
from Melodie, a tub of glittery lip gloss
from Grace, a silk bag of sweets from
Honey, a pack of magic playing cards
from Polly and a sparkly bracelet from
Phoebe. And Jasmine had given them
each a golden jewellery box with a
revolving fairy on top to put all their
presents in.

Rachel and Kirsty couldn't believe their eyes.

"We must be the luckiest girls in the world," Rachel sighed.

"And we can still enjoy the rest of the street party, too," Kirsty added.

Later that night, the girls lay in their beds in Kirsty's room, still too excited to sleep. The jewellery boxes, filled with presents, sat on the dressing-table.

"It's sad that I have to go home tomorrow," Rachel said with a yawn. "But I've really enjoyed our latest fairy adventure and we'll see each other again soon?"

"Me too," Kirsty agreed, starting to feel sleepy at last. She closed her eyes.

There was silence for a few moments. Then, "I can hear something," Rachel said. "It's coming from our jewellery boxes!"

The soft, tinkling sound of party music filled the room.

"Fairy magic!" Kirsty said happily, snuggling down under her duvet. "Goodnight, Rachel."

Win a Rainbow Magic
Sparkly T-Shirt and Goody Bag!

In every book in the Rainbow Magic Party Fairies series (books 15–21) there is a hidden picture of a magic party bag with a secret letter in it. Find all seven letters and re-arrange them to make a special Fairyland word, then send it to us. Each month we will put the entries into a draw and select one winner to receive a Rainbow Magic Sparkly T-shirt and Goody Bag!

Send your entry on a postcard to Rainbow Magic Competition, Orchard Books, 96 Leonard Street, London EC2A 4XD. Australian readers should write to Level 17/207 Kent St, Sydney, NSW 2000. Don't forget to include your name and address. Only one entry per child. Final draw: 28th April 2006.

Coming Soon...
The Jewel Fairies

INDIA THE MOONSTONE FAIRY
1-84362-958-5

SCARLETT THE GARNET FAIRY   1-84362-954-2

EMILY THE EMERALD FAIRY
1-84362-955-0

CHLOE THE TOPAZ FAIRY
1-84362-956-9

AMY THE AMETHYST FAIRY
1-84362-957-7

SOPHIE THE SAPPHIRE FAIRY
1-84362-953-4

LUCY THE DIAMOND FAIRY
1-84362-959-3

Also coming soon . . .

SUMMER THE HOLIDAY FAIRY
1-84362-638-1

Summer the Holiday Fairy is getting all hot and
bothered, trying to keep Rainspell Island the best
place to go on vacation. Jack Frost has stolen the
sand from the beaches, and three magical shells.
The fairies need Rachel and Kirsty's help
to get the holiday magic back...

Have you checked out the

Website at:

www.rainbowmagic.co.uk

There are games, activities and fun things to do, as well as news and information about Rainbow Magic and all of the fairies.

RAINBOW magic

by Daisy Meadows

Ruby the Red Fairy	ISBN	1 84362 016 2
Amber the Orange Fairy	ISBN	1 84362 017 0
Saffron the Yellow Fairy	ISBN	1 84362 018 9
Fern the Green Fairy	ISBN	1 84362 019 7
Sky the Blue Fairy	ISBN	1 84362 020 0
Izzy the Indigo Fairy	ISBN	1 84362 021 9
Heather the Violet Fairy	ISBN	1 84362 022 7

The Weather Fairies

Crystal the Snow Fairy	ISBN	1 84362 633 0
Abigail the Breeze Fairy	ISBN	1 84362 634 9
Pearl the Cloud Fairy	ISBN	1 84362 635 7
Goldie the Sunshine Fairy	ISBN	1 84362 641 1
Evie the Mist Fairy	ISBN	1 84362 636 5
Storm the Lightning Fairy	ISBN	1 84362 637 3
Hayley the Rain Fairy	ISBN	1 84362 638 1

The Party Fairies

Cherry the Cake Fairy	ISBN	1 84362 818 X
Melodie the Music Fairy	ISBN	1 84362 819 8
Grace the Glitter Fairy	ISBN	1 84362 820 1
Honey the Sweet Fairy	ISBN	1 84362 821 X
Polly the Party Fun Fairy	ISBN	1 84362 822 8
Phoebe the Fashion Fairy	ISBN	1 84362 823 6
Jasmine the Present Fairy	ISBN	1 84362 824 4
Holly the Christmas Fairy	ISBN	1 84362 661 6

All priced at £3.99. Holly the Christmas Fairy priced at £4.99.
Rainbow Magic books are available from all good bookshops, or can be ordered
direct from the publisher: Orchard Books, PO BOX 29, Douglas IM99 1BQ
Credit card orders please telephone 01624 836000
or fax 01624 837033 or visit our Internet site: www.wattspub.co.uk
or e-mail: bookshop@enterprise.net for details.

To order please quote title, author and ISBN and your full name and address.
Cheques and postal orders should be made payable to 'Bookpost plc.'
Postage and packing is FREE within the UK
(overseas customers should add £2.00 per book).
Prices and availability are subject to change.